HERE COMES THE CAT ! / СЮДА ИДЕТ КОТ !

FRANK ASCH   VLADIMIR VAGIN

SCHOLASTIC INC.

NEW YORK TORONTO LONDON
AUCKLAND SYDNEY

ISBN 0-590-41854-8

Copyright © 1989 by Frank Asch & Vladimir Vagin.
All rights reserved. Published by Scholastic Inc.
BLUE RIBBON is a registered trademark of Scholastic Inc.

12 11 10 9 8 7 6 5 4 3   1 2 3 4 5 6/9

Printed in the U.S.A.   23

In Russian,
СЮДА ИДЕТ КОТ!
means *Here Comes the Cat!*
and is pronounced
syu-DAH ee-DYOT KOT!

To my son,   To my daughter,
DEVIN   NASTIYA
—FRANK ASCH   —VLADIMIR VAGIN